Let's Play Tag!

 Read the Page

Say It   Sound It   Spell It

★ Game

↻ Repeat

◻ Stop

Why is wh yellow?

Yellow highlights represent letter teams
that make a single sound or words
with irregular decoding patterns.

At the Lake in June

Story by Suzanne Barchers
Illustrated by Randy Chewning
Designed by Six Red Marbles

 June is here at last. The sun is so hot.

"Let's go to the
lake!" says Jude.
"We like it a lot!"

"Can Duke go, too?" says Luke. "He will have such fun."

Duke likes to run
over the huge dunes
and then nap in
the sun.

 "You know the rules!" says Mom. "First, get your chores done."

"Let's clean up this mess. Then we can go have fun."

Luke has a huge job. But Jude helps him, too.

Even Duke helps.
There's lots he
can do.

Jude has a cute suit. Luke gets a huge tube.

Mom fixes snacks.
Even Duke will want
food!

 They pack up the car. Duke gets in the back.

Luke sits next to
Duke, and Jude puts
in the snack.

As they ride to the lake, Luke and Jude sing a cute tune.

In no time at all,
they see the lake
and sand dunes.

 Jude grabs her raft.
Luke uses his tube.

Duke runs for the
dunes. Mom pours
juice and adds
ice cubes.

Dad sings a tune as he strums on his lute.

Mom hums the tune
and then plays on
her flute.

 "It's snack time,"
says Mom.
"Let's sit here,"
says Luke.

"No, I want to sit there," says Jude. "Come on, Duke."

They all look at Dad. He says, "I will not have a dispute."

"Okay," say Jude
and Luke as they
give Dad a salute.

It's time to go
on this fine day in
June. They wave
goodbye as Duke
howls a tune.

pole

rope

dune

flute

lute

tune

Luke

Jude

slope

bone

nose

tube

cone

robe

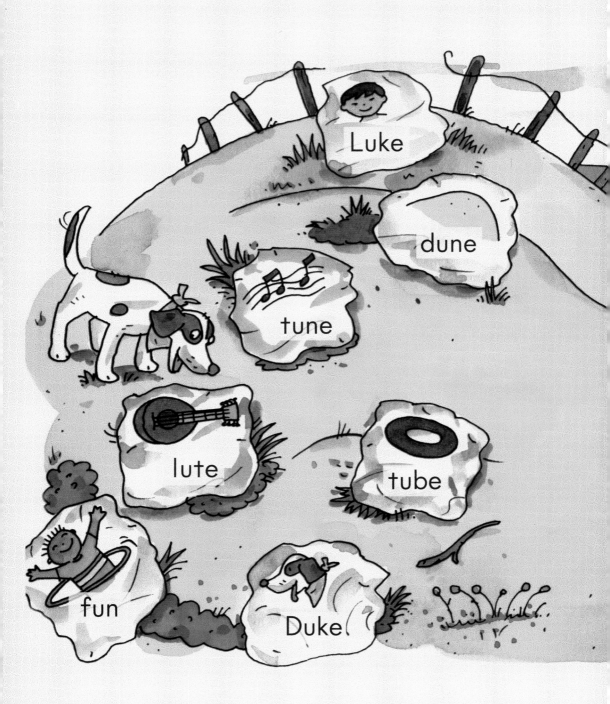

Luke

dune

tune

lute

tube

fun

Duke

run

back

cube

sun

flute

June

snack

cute

Words You're Learning

Long Vowels, Silent E & Y

Skill Words

cubes	dunes	June	salute
cute	flute	Luke	tube
dispute	huge	lute	tune
Duke	Jude	rules	uses

Sight Words

all	done	it's
as	here	says
come		

Challenging Words

car	give	plays	such
chores	goodbye	pours	suit
clean	howls	say	then
day	juice	sing	there's
even	no	sings	this
first	okay	so	too
food	over	strums	